D0509496

First published 2002 by Walker Books Ltd
87 Vauxhall Walk, London SE11 5HJ
2 4 6 8 10 9 7 5 3 1
© 2002 Universal Pictures Visual Programming Ltd
™Sitting Ducks Productions
Licensed by Universal Studios Licensing LLLP
Printed in Spain
All rights reserved
British Library Cataloguing in Publication Data:
a catalogue record for this book is available
from the British Library
ISBN 0-7445-8948-7

Duck Naked!

Story by Danielle Mentzer
Adapted by Charlie Gardner

"AAAAAAAAAAAAAAAAAAAAAAGH!"
Something terrible was happening to Bill, and he didn't know why.

The morning had started innocently enough – when Bill woke up, he'd found a few loose feathers on his pillow and thought nothing of it. But when he got out of the shower, and looked in the mirror, he was horrified: he was covered in huge pink patches where his feathers used to be.

"AAAAAAAAAAAAAAAAAAAAAGH!"
Bill ran into the sitting-room, a jet-trail of white feathers fluttering in his wake. "Help me, I'm coming undone!"

Aldo looked round the door in amazement. Was Bill trying some new morning exercises, perhaps?

Boom, Boom! Aldo bounded in smiling. But when he saw Bill close up, his eyes leapt out on stalks.

"Don't come near me!" screamed Bill, trying to hide himself. "I might be contagious!"

Just then, Ed, Oly and Waddle turned up.

"Wow, Bill, you're having a really bad feather day," said Waddle, in shock.

"Tell me it's not some hideous disease," pleaded Bill. "I'm too young to die!"

"You're not dying – you're losing your old feathers!" Ed laughed. "They will grow back again ... eventually..."

Aldo still didn't understand. "OK," he grimaced, "who plucked my little buddy?"

"Nobody," replied Bill. He trembled and a few more feathers fell out. "Aldo, I'm ... I'm ... I'm moulting!"

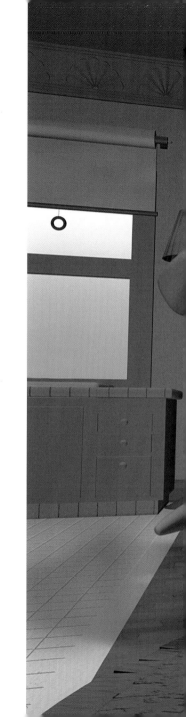

Aldo looked puzzled.

"Moulting? Is there anything you can do about it?"

"Rent a lot of videos and wait for the new feathers to grow in?" Ed suggested.

"I can't wait," sobbed Bill. "THIS IS THE WORST DAY OF MY LIFE!"

Aldo helped Bill collect his feathers while Ed hurriedly scribbled on some paper. "Follow this map," he whispered in Bill's ear. "Knock on the back door five times and say 'The naked bird has landed'. There's a friend inside who can fix you up..."

"You guys have tried this, right?" Bill worried.

"Only once," replied Oly, embarrassed. "It was a bad year."

"And is it safe?"

"Er ... mostly." Ed hesitated. "Just make sure you're not followed..."

"You'll be OK," smiled Aldo. "I'm coming with you..."

Bill and Aldo made an unlikely looking pair as they sped through the streets of Ducktown. Bill steered the scooter skilfully through the busy streets and back alleys, slowing down a little now and again to make sure no one was trailing the tell-tale stream of feathers behind them.

"I think we're lost!" Bill yelled.

"Try the next turn," Aldo ventured, struggling with the map.

They sped past Bill's apartment block. Bill stopped the scooter a few blocks down.

"We *are* lost," he grimaced. "That's the second time we've been past my apartment!"

"But I've been following the map the whole time," said Aldo, meekly.

"Following the map ... upside down! Here, let me have it..."

Bill started the bike and zoomed off, making a quick left turn and then a quick right before screeching to a halt outside the familiar front of the Decoy Café.

Bill parked the scooter. "This is the place," he said confidently.

"Great idea," Aldo grinned. "I could do with a snack."

Bill's state of undress was already attracting unwelcome hoots of laughter. Aldo hurried him along a passage leading to a heavy steel door. Bill knocked tentatively.

"Vot is the passvurt?" demanded a strange female voice from behind the door.

"The naked bird has landed," Bill replied hurriedly.

"The vot bird?"

"The naked bird!"

"Zo zorry, I am haffink trouble hearink you."

"THE NAKED PLUCKED TOTALLY FEATHERLESS BIRD HAS LANDED!"

With a clang, the door swung open.

Aldo and Bill stood in the doorway. The room was dark and cavernous. In the centre, a single light bulb swung menacingly over a large, round table.

"Please take a seat," said the foreign voice from somewhere in the darkness. Hesitantly, Bill and Aldo sat at the table, and after a few moments a strange, yet familiar figure stepped into the light.

"I am Madame Bevousky," said the gypsy-like bird before them.

"No you're not, you're Bev!" Bill spluttered. And certainly there was more than a passing resemblance to the owner of the Decoy Café.

"Nothing is as it appears," Madame Bev continued confidently, then whispered, "You must believe. The cure depends on it." There was an expectant hush in the room as Madame Bev produced a small glass tube. The liquid inside glowed strangely in the downlight.

"Bill, are you ready to be transformed?"

"Er … I think so," hesitated Bill, getting to his feet.

Madame Bev uncorked the tube and held it menacingly above Bill's shining dome.

"With this tiny drop I pour, may my friend Bill be plucked no more!" Bill shut his eyes tight. There was a moment's silence and then, POP, POP, POP! Bill's remaining feathers hit the ground faster than a falling tree!

"Oh my!" Madame Bev exclaimed in a Bev-like voice. "That's never happened before! You must have had an allergic reaction."

"Do something!" yelled Bill, "I'M DUCK NAKED!"

"We must use more powerful magic." Still calm, Bev threw back a large curtain. "Behold, the Mystical Mallard Makeover Machine!"

Standing before them was a huge hairdryer attached to a comfy leather chair. Bill was uneasy — this thing had wires coming out of it like spaghetti.

"Is there another way?" he gulped.

"No," replied Bev abruptly.

Bill climbed into the chair and held on tight. "Just turn it on then," he burbled.

Bev flicked a switch and the machine coughed into action. Sparks flew as the dryer whirred and vibrated like a runaway spin-dryer. Smoke started to rise from the hood — but at that precise moment Bev hit the STOP switch. Bill looked at himself — he was covered in beautiful white feathers.

"I'm back to normal, I'm back to normal!" Bill jumped for joy.

"Oops! Missed a bit," groaned Bev.

Aldo showed Bill what was missing. "Your rear's a feather-free zone, little buddy!"

"I'm going back in," Bill said through gritted beak.

"Oh no," Bev worried. "Strange things can happen if you go in twice..."

Too late, the little duck was upside down in the chair, his tail facing the hood, as the machine spluttered into action.

"Did it work?" asked Bill hopefully, a few seconds after the eider-enhancer had ground to a halt. Aldo's eyes were as big as saucers.

"You might say that..." he grinned.

Bill looked in the mirror.

"I'M GREEN!"

"It could have been worse," laughed Bev. "Oly turned purple! Anyway, it will wash out in a week!"

Later that evening, Bill and Aldo chilled out on the balcony.

"You know, little buddy," mused Aldo. "I really like your luminous plumage."

Bill was seriously unimpressed.

"No really, those fluorescent feathers might start a fashion!"

"Next time, I think I will just stay in and watch movies," Bill dreamed. "After all, I am a duck — moulting happens." He stared up at the stars, then added, "You know, it's not so bad being green…"

"I never thought so," grinned Aldo.

Then the two friends picked up their bongos and began a bossa-nova beat that drifted away into the night.